4/09

Teatime

in

Space

Published in the United States by
QEB Publishing, Inc.
23062 La Cadena Drive
Laguna Hills, CA 92653

www.qeb-publishing.com

Library of Congress Control Number: 2008011789

ISBN 978 1 59566 574 4

Printed and bound in the United States

Author Caroline Castle
Illustrator Paul Nicholls
Editor Clare Weaver
Designer Alix Wood
Consultant Anne Faundez

Publisher Steve Evans
Creative Director Zeta Davies

Teatime in Space

Caroline Castle

Illustrated by

Paul Nicholls

QEB Publishing

One afternoon, a spaceship landed in Pete's backyard in a shower of sparks.

"Wow!"
said Pete.

A small, green creature climbed down.

"Greetings, pink one,"
said the creature.
"I am Zub of Planet Flub."

"Greetings, green one," said Pete.
"I am Pete of Planet Earth."

"Can you help me?" said Zub.
"My Flubmobile has broken
down. Mombo of Zub will be
very cross if I am late for tea."

Pete examined the little spaceship.
Zub showed him the controls.

Starter

Flubmobile

Fuel

Zoomer

Really
fast

Faster

Slow

Pete saw the problem at once.
The down button was stuck.

He **wiggled** it and he **waggled** it.

But then...

Backward **Forward**

Zigzag

Hover

Up

Down

The little spaceship took off.

Zoom

All of a sudden, they were in outer space!

"Oh, no!" cried Pete.
"Quick, let's push the down button again!"

Pete and Zub pushed the button
as hard as they could.
But the spaceship
just zoomed higher and
higher and higher.

"Oh, no!" cried Pete. "Mombo of Pete will be very angry.
It's my teatime soon, and I'm not allowed to go beyond the
backyard gate. Let alone into outer space!"

"Sorry," said Zub.
"But it's on autopilot.
Any minute now, we will be on Planet Flub."

At that very moment,

the little spaceship landed–**bump!**–on Planet Flub.

Mombo of Zub came rushing from the house.
She was not pleased.

"Naughty Zub!" she cried. "You know you are
not allowed to go beyond the backyard stars.
And who is this strange pink creature?"

Zub told Mombo all about his
adventure on Planet Earth, and
how Pete had helped him to
repair the little spaceship.

Mombo of Zub was
so grateful to Pete,
she invited him to tea.

Pete looked at his watch. Mombo of Pete would be
calling him in ten minutes. There was just enough time.

They had zoogle fingers,

and waffle tops on
wobble plates,

and a glass
of google juice.

Then Pete said he really must go.

Pete said goodbye to Flub,
then Mombo of Zub
flew him home—zap!
—in her Superzoom Zippership.

He arrived just in time for tea on Planet Earth.

It was fish fingers on brown toast with a glass of fizzy orange.

Pete wasn't the least bit hungry.

But he ate it
all up anyway.

After all, he could hardly tell Mom
that he had already had his tea...

—in **space!**

Notes for teachers and parents

- Look at the front cover of the book together. Talk about the picture. Can the children guess what the story is going to be about? Read the title together.

- When the children first read the story (or had it read to them), how did they think the story was going to end? Were they right? Discuss other ideas of how the story might have ended.

- Ask the children to take it in turns to try to read the story aloud. Help them with any difficult words and remember to praise the children for their efforts in reading the book.

- Explain that the Earth is a planet, too. Can the children name any other planets? Look at a picture of the solar system and ask the children if they can find Earth. Point out and name the other major planets. Zub's Planet Flub is too small to feature on the picture! Ask the children to choose a location for Planet Flub (not too far away from Earth!).

- Is there life in space? Many people think they have seen flying saucers, but it has never been proved so we just don't know! Encourage the children to invent their own space creatures —what might they look like, and what would they be called? Get them to draw pictures of their creatures and design a spaceship of their own.

- In pairs, the children can take on the roles of Pete and Flub, and act out the dialog throughout the book.

- Although Pete and Flub come from different planets, they both have families who do the same things! Discuss with the children why both Pete and Flub are not allowed beyond the backyard gate/backyard stars on their own. For example, they might get lost (which is exactly what happened to Flub!), or have an accident.

- Pete and Flub eat very different food! Discuss what types of different food children eat in other parts of the world. What might children have for tea in India or China, for instance?

- Ask the children, with a parent, to look at the night sky just before bedtime. Explain that they may be able to see the stars and the Moon. Discuss with them the fact that humans have landed on the Moon, and perhaps one day life will be found in space.